Rumpelstiltskin

Story by:
Wilhelm and Jacob Grimm

Adapted by:
Margaret Ann Hughes

Illustrated by:

Russell Hicks	Lorann Downer
Theresa Mazurek	Rivka
Douglas McCarthy	Fay Whitemountain
Allyn Conley-Gorniak	Suzanne Lewis
Julie Ann Armstrong	Lisa Souza

This Book Belongs To:

Victoria and Jennifer Whiston

Use this symbol to match book and cassette.

Once upon a time there was a poor miller who lived with his beautiful daughter, Melinda, in a tiny little house. The miller worked and worked in his old mill, but times were hard, and they were growing poorer and poorer by the day. Finally, he decided he would go to the king and ask to borrow some money.

The miller kissed his daughter "goodbye" and set out on foot toward the castle. There he was given permission to see the king.

As the miller walked down the long aisle to the king's throne, he overheard the king talking to his minister about finding a queen.

Without thinking, the miller boldly stepped up to the king and told him about his very own daughter, Melinda.

The miller, desperate to interest him in his daughter, told the king that Melinda could spin straw into gold!

The king was quite interested in meeting a girl who could make gold out of straw.

And so, the miller was ordered to bring Melinda to the castle at once.

The miller returned home and told Melinda that she, his daughter, was to meet…the king!

Melinda was very excited! That night, the miller returned to the castle with his daughter and introduced her to the king. He was pleased with her beauty.

But both the king and the miller knew why he was really interested in Melinda.

The king escorted Melinda down a long hall to a small room. The miller and the king's minister followed.

He opened the door to the small room. It was filled with piles of straw. And in the middle of the room sat a spinning wheel.

The king wanted Melinda to spin the straw into gold!

Melinda didn't know what to say. Her father certainly put her in a difficult situation. To make gold out of straw would be impossible, but all she could do was try.

The king told Melinda that she had until morning to spin all the straw into gold. Then he quickly ushered everyone else out of the room.

Melinda sat on a pile of straw and looked around her. There were no windows and only one door. And everywhere she looked, there were piles and piles of straw.

Just then, a little man magically appeared in the room. He wore a funny crooked hat, and he had a very bad temper!

Melinda explained how she had to spin all the straw into gold by morning.

Unpleasantly, the little man said that he would help Melinda spin all the straw into gold, if she would give him something valuable in return.

Sadly, Melinda gave the little man her necklace. Then he sat down at the spinning wheel and began to spin. Melinda watched in amazement as the strands of straw turned into beautiful gold.

While the little man worked long into the night, Melinda slept on a pile of straw.

The next morning, the king entered the room and
found the miller's daughter sleeping on a pile of gold.
The entire room was filled with piles of gold!
The king was pleasantly surprised!

Then the king ushered Melinda to another room, twice as
large as the first and had it filled with twice as much straw.
If she could spin all that straw into gold, the king would
make her his queen.

Once again the king left Melinda alone
to make gold out of straw.

Just then, the little man with the funny crooked hat appeared again.

The little man said he would spin the straw into gold one last time, if Melinda gave him something even more valuable than before.

The little man knew that the king would marry the miller's daughter, so he asked her to give him her first born child. Melinda couldn't even think about the future, with the task left before her. So she quickly agreed to give him her first child.

He sat down to work and spun the straw into gold once again, while Melinda slept.

When the king arrived in the morning, he was pleased to find Melinda sleeping on a pile of gold, as before.

And so, the king and the miller's daughter were married, and the miller was given a place at the castle to live. As time passed, the king and queen were blessed with the birth of a son.

Now one day, while the queen was alone with her baby, the little man with the funny crooked hat magically appeared to take the child she had promised.

The queen had forgotten her promise, and she begged him to reconsider.

The little man gave the queen a chance to save her child. In three days she must guess the little man's name. If she succeeded, he would not take her child.

Then the little man disappeared. He would return at sunset the next day.

The queen immediately sent out three servants to search the countryside for information about the little man. She had only three days to discover his name.

The servants returned the first day with nothing to report. Then, as the sun was setting, the little man appeared to see if Melinda could guess his name.

Melinda tried every name she could think of, but not one was right.

And so, the little man quickly disappeared, to return at sunset the next day.

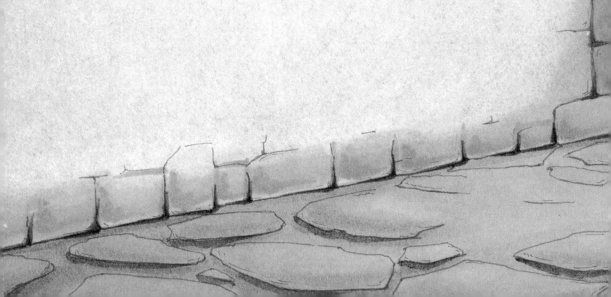

The following morning, the queen sent out even more servants to find something, anything about the little man, hoping to discover his name. But again they came back with nothing to report. As the sun set, the little man returned. And the guessing began again.

Again and again Melinda guessed names, but not one of them was right.

Then the little man disappeared, quite confident that Melinda would never guess his name.

It was the morning of the last day. Melinda decided that she, herself, must discover the little man's name. She mounted her horse and rode out into the countryside.

As Melinda rode through the forest, she crossed a brook. Suddenly she remembered that the little man had mentioned a babbling brook.

As she followed the brook, she then remembered
him mentioning chattering squirrels.

Following the brook farther, Melinda came to a little
house, surrounded by families of squirrels!

Melinda was certain she had found his house. Then
she saw the little man dancing and singing in his
garden. She moved in closer and listened.

Rumpelstiltskin was his name! Quickly Melinda
rode out of the forest and back to the castle.

Just as the sun began to set, the little man appeared at the castle one last time to see if the queen could guess his name.

Melinda knew his name and told him so. Therefore the little man couldn't take her child.

Well, Rumpelstiltskin was furious that the queen had guessed his name. He stomped his foot so hard that he fell right through the floor, and was never seen again! Melinda hadn't really guessed Rumpelstiltskin's name. She just took the time to remember what he, himself, had said. And so, she figured it out, herself.

And they all lived happily ever after.